A KISS UNDER THE NORTHERN LIGHTS

ROSE MARIE MEUWISSEN

ISBN: 978-0-9903788-8-4
Published in the United States of America
Nordic Publishing
Edited by Nancy Schumacher
Cover Design by Rose Marie Meuwissen

nordic
PUBLISHING

❀ Created with Vellum

To all those who dream of seeing the Northern Lights someday,
may your dream come true.

INTRODUCTION

A MINNESOTA LAKES ROMANCE
NOVELETTE

Big Lake

Bailey is at a crossroads...

Does she give up her life-long goal of becoming a top photographer or keep pressing on, hoping to make an exceptional portfolio of the Northern Lights? Booking a room at the Northern Lights Resort in Ely, Minnesota is her last resort. If she can get some great shots of the northern lights, she may be able to revive her career. If not, she'll be forced to seek a boring desk job in corporate America. Alex, her tour guide, isn't what she's expecting, but maybe he's just what she needs.

Alex has given up on finding the woman of his dreams...

He's desperate to meet a woman who'll love him for the man he is outside the boardroom, not just the CEO of a multi-million-dollar clothing company. Getting away for a few weeks to help his parents at the family's resort is just what he needs to clear his head and think about his next steps. Acting as a tour guide for a fearful city gal isn't part of his plan, but sometimes when you least expect it, love comes calling.

A MINNESOTA LAKES ROMANCE

MINNESOTA

Land of 10,000 Lakes

A KISS UNDER THE NORTHERN LIGHTS

by

Rose Marie Meuwissen

CHAPTER 1

"*Y*ou're going where?" Brigitte asked her daughter.

"Ely, Minnesota." Bailey knew her mother would have a difficult time understanding the driving need she had to photograph pictures of the Northern Lights.

"You hate the outdoors."

This was true, Bailey mused, as thoughts of bears and wolves overwhelmed her. Who's afraid of them, anyway? Bailey Sandberg certainly was! So why had she booked a trip to Ely, Minnesota to spend two weeks in the wild to see if she could luck out and get fabulous pictures of the Northern Lights? Photography had been her passion ever since she'd acquired a camera on her 10th birthday. It was an immediate love of photos. And, oh, how photography had changed since then. Who would've ever thought fabulous pictures could be taken with a phone? Her brand-new EOS-1D X Mark II camera with multiple lenses was incredible. And the clarity was unbelievable. She loved it!

Bailey recognized her mother was only concerned for her. She was a city girl through and through. "I'm sure I can survive two weeks in northern Minnesota. How bad can it be? They do have electricity and bathrooms. Wi-Fi may be a bit shaky."

"How about cell service? Don't think you can live off the grid."

"Of course, I can. Do I want to? No, but if that's what it takes for me to get incredible photos of the Northern Lights, I'm willing to make the sacrifice."

After graduating from the Minneapolis College of Art and Design with a degree in photography, she'd worked internships for local portrait studios. Then she'd worked for small wedding photography businesses, all the while gaining experience and learning the ropes.

On her twenty-seventh birthday, she'd decided it was time to start her own photography business. What she really wanted was to take incredibly beautiful photos of unusual scenes. The main part she was lacking was customers. Unfortunately, she'd had to market to the wedding clientele to pay the bills. Not that she didn't like weddings, but it just wasn't satisfying her creative side.

So, when she saw an ad in the Minnesota Explorer's summer magazine for trips to the far northern part of Minnesota to see the Northern Lights, she was intrigued. Seeing them was something she'd always dreamed of doing. The Northern Lights were considered a phenomenon only visible in a few parts of the world. Scandinavia including Iceland, Canada, Minnesota, and Alaska were the best places to see them. Luckily, she lived in Minnesota.

"I give you a week tops." Brigitte gave Bailey her 'mother is always right' look.

"One more thing. You always said if I needed to move back home for any reason..."

Brigitte walked over to give her daughter a motherly hug.

"I did. And you can stay as long as you need to. Just need a couple of days to get the loft apartment cleaned up."

"Thanks, Mom. I was thinking this weekend."

"Perfect. It will be nice to have my baby back."

"Hopefully, the Northern Lights pictures will be just what I need to jumpstart my business."

"You know your dad and I are always willing to do whatever it takes to help you succeed and make your dreams come true."

"You guys are the best parents ever!"

"Just one thing. We need to go shopping. You're going to need some clothing made for the outdoors. Even in the summer it can be chilly up north. I've read about a new line of clothing designed for the weather conditions in that part of Minnesota. If I recall correctly, it's called, Below Zero."

"I probably need to do that. How about after I get moved in next week?"

"Great! And I'm buying."

"Mom…"

"Consider it a birthday gift."

Bailey had blocked off the two weeks in July after the 4th of July holiday and booked a stay at the Northern Lights Resort in Ely, Minnesota. She'd picked it because they offered guided tours to see the phenomenon. And with a name like that how could she go wrong? Usually, this incredible spectacle of lights was unpredictable and occurred in the middle of the night, which could present a problem.

She was not an outdoors woman by any means. In fact, she immensely disliked the wilderness of Minnesota. It was filled with mosquitos, wood ticks, bears, wolves and various other critters—all of which frightened her, and she truly hated being scared. You might think mosquitos were nothing to be afraid of, and although they probably wouldn't kill you, they could make you very sick. Lyme's disease was nothing to take lightly. But if she wanted the pictures, she would have to live through her fears. Even if it meant going out at night into the woods filled with wild animals, she was determined to get the pictures of a lifetime. She only hoped her guide would be able to protect her from her own fears and the wild creatures of the night.

CHAPTER 2

*A*lex Schneider loved the dynamics of life in Minneapolis. Of course, that didn't mean he didn't like life in his hometown of Ely. In fact, he was unable to decide which he liked best. Both had their pluses and he loved them equally. He fell in love with Minneapolis after he moved there to attend the University of Minnesota to earn a Business Degree.

Starting a clothing company hadn't been on his goal list. It just happened. He'd acquired first-hand knowledge of the weather in Northern Minnesota by spending his youth in the outdoor elements, giving him a good idea of what was needed in outdoor clothing today to keep people warm under those extreme winter conditions. Luckily, he'd been introduced to a talented woman who could create clothing products from his crazy, incoherent drawings that looked more like doodling. His clothing line, Below Zero, helped people maintain their preferable body temperature in light-weight, comfortable and attractive outdoor gear.

But when his mother, Ursula, called to ask him to help

out at the family's Northern Lights Resort for the month of July, he'd seized the opportunity for a long overdue vacation.

The drive to Ely was over four hours from Minneapolis. It was one he'd driven many times, usually stopping in Duluth on the way for lunch. The weather was great, in fact almost perfect—sunny with clear skies and about seventy-five degrees. He couldn't wait to see his parents and his sister, Renate, who handled all the finances and marketing for the resort. The closer he drove, the more wooded and hilly the landscape became. He loved it up north and it had been way too long since he'd been back home.

He parked in front of the main lodge building which housed the reception area and offices along with the restaurant. His SUV was loaded with boxes of Below Zero gear to restock the gift shop in the lodge.

The resort consisted of the main lodge with twenty-four rooms. Closer to the lake were twelve, two-bedroom cabins. Recently, they'd added two larger, luxury cabins that had four bedrooms and all the amenities. The family had built a large home for themselves, complete with almost all windows facing the lake, up on the hill behind the lodge. The breathtaking view stretched for miles across the water. Fond memories of growing up on Big Lake surfaced.

"Alex, you're home!" said his mother, Ursula, as she ran up to embrace him.

"Hello, Mother," he answered giving her a quick kiss on the cheek.

"It's good to see you, son," greeted his father, Peter, walking up behind his mother to shake his hand.

"It's good to be home. I've been looking forward to this vacation." He laughed. "It is a vacation, isn't it?"

His mother smiled at him. "Now that you're here, we will be putting you to work."

"I'm all yours for the rest of the month. What do you need help with?"

"I was trying to drum up some extra business, and I guess it worked," Renate stated, joining them in the lobby.

"I guess that's good, sis. So, what do you need me to do?"

"If you could handle the fishing excursions that would be a huge help. Dad hurt his back so getting in and out of the boats has been an issue."

"It really sucks to get old," his dad said, rubbing his lower back.

"No problem. I come to work, and you send me out to fish. Piece of cake!"

"There's one other thing." Renate hesitated before continuing. "I advertised night excursions to see the Northern Lights."

"Really? How does that work?"

"Not quite sure, but somebody booked one. She will be here on Saturday and is staying for two weeks."

"Two weeks?"

"Well, you know the Northern Lights are unpredictable and she wants to be sure she gets to see them. She's a photographer from Minneapolis. Her company is called, In Focus."

"Great! You want me to babysit some city gal for two weeks? You need to be outside in the middle of the night to see them—"

"I know. Hopefully, we'll get lucky and she will get some great shots right away and leave early."

"You better not have saddled me with some city snob for two weeks!"

"Enough! I have a feeling everything will work out just fine. No fighting. Peter, show Alex around the boat house." She motioned for Alex and Peter to leave through the front door. "We have a new boat. I think you will like it."

"Renate, you could've waited till after dinner," Ursula remarked to her daughter.

"Best to get it over with now. Who knows? Maybe she'll turn out to be a hot chick, and he'll love every minute he spends with her." Renate laughed as her mother shooed her back to the office.

CHAPTER 3

*B*ailey knew Ely was near the Canadian border, she just didn't realize how many hours of driving it would take her to get there. From Savage, a southern suburb of Minneapolis, it took about five hours. After a couple of bathroom breaks caused by all the coffee she'd been drinking, and a lunch stop, she finally saw the sign for Ely. Luckily her phone GPS was still working as she would need its help to find the resort, which was out of town a bit.

As she drove down Main Street, all the quaint little shops came into view. There was a restaurant called Brittons Café, which she'd read about online. They were known for their pancakes, large enough to fill a whole dinner plate. She'd definitely have to stop back for breakfast one day.

The Dorothy Molter Museum, where one could buy Dorothy's famous root beer, appeared at the end of the street. Dorothy was a strong, independent woman from the early 1900s who, along with being a nurse, was an entrepreneur producing her own root beer line known as Dorothy's Isle of Pines Root Beer. From what she'd read online, she couldn't wait to sample the root beer.

Next, she spotted the Rockwood Bar and Grill. It had received high praise for its made-from-scratch, new style offerings complete with live music. She loved live music, but wasn't a fan of going alone, which was why she hadn't been to any music events recently. Maybe she would be brave and try going alone.

The signage for the International Wolf Center and the North American Bear Center appeared at the end of town. From what she'd heard about them, she wasn't so sure she wanted to go there. One of her worst fears was wild animals like wolves and bears, so why would she want to go see some? They were relatively common in this area, making her wary to be outside of the lodge after sunset.

Finally, she saw the Northern Lights Resort sign ahead on the left. She turned and followed the winding dirt road and pulled into the small parking lot in front of the lodge. It felt so good to get out of the car and stretch her legs. She liked what she saw. A lodge built with cedar logs and a new metal style green roof. It blended perfectly with the pine and oak tree forest surrounding it. Grabbing her purse, she went to check in at the front desk.

She was greeted by a beautiful young woman. "Good afternoon and welcome to Northern Lights Resort. I'm Renate, how can I help you?"

"I'm checking in. My name is Bailey Sandberg."

"We're glad you chose our resort. I have you in one of our new cabins. I think you'll like it. You'll have a picture-perfect view of the lake."

"Thanks."

"Alex will be your guide for the Northern Lights tour. I'll have him stop by later to introduce himself."

"That's great. Can I ask you a question about the tour?"

"Sure."

"How safe is this tour? Should I be worried?"

"Alex is my brother and I'm sure he'll be a perfect gentleman," Renate stated confidently.

"Oh, that's not what I meant. So sorry to insinuate anything about your brother. I meant I'm just deathly afraid of bears and wolves."

"Well, that is something totally different. Let me reassure you, Alex grew up here, so he knows these woods like the back of his hand. He knows how to deal with bears and wolves, if, by chance you run into any, which you probably won't."

"Are you sure?"

"It's been a few years since I've seen a bear and even longer since I've seen any wolves. Usually you only see them at dusk if they are looking for food. But trust me, there is plenty of wild food for them to eat in these woods and in the lake. You'll be fine."

"Okay. I really am looking forward to getting some pictures of the Northern Lights."

"You know we can't guarantee it, but July is a prime month for seeing them, so your chances are good."

"I hope so," Bailey said.

"Here is your key and a map of the resort," Renate said and gave her a reassuring smile.

Bailey pulled up to the cutest little cabin and smiled. The lake view was fabulous, and if she didn't acquire any pictures of the Northern Lights she could at least get some great lake and nature photos.

She unpacked and got settled into her little home for the next two weeks. The kitchen boasted granite counters and top-of-the-line appliances. There were two bedrooms, so she took the master bedroom and put her photo equipment in the other bedroom.

It was six o'clock and she was famished. She hadn't eaten since lunchtime, so she decided to go up to the lodge and have dinner. Tomorrow she would make a trip into town to buy some groceries. She was on a tight budget, which meant she'd be cooking most of her own meals. Actually, she should be cooking all of them and not going out to eat at all, but she'd been driving all day, or at least it seemed like it anyway, and she didn't have enough energy left to drive back into town. She decided to treat herself tonight and set aside some money to go to Brittons Café, the Rockwood Bar and Grill and to also pick up some of the famous root beer in Ely.

Being flush with money was not in her near future. In fact, she had very little left after booking the trip, which was why she'd moved back in with her parents. This trip was her last chance to save her business. If this didn't jump start it, she'd have to get a minimum wage office job and try to work her way up from the bottom. She loved photography. It was what made her feel alive and happy.

She heard a knock at the door. The man she saw through the window was gorgeous, if you could even call men that. His blond hair was full and combed back. His body looked firm and fit in the tight jeans and body hugging shirt he filled out perfectly. He was not gorgeous, he was hot.

"Hello," she said as she opened the door and looked into baby blue eyes.

"Hi, my name is Alex. I'll be your tour guide for the Northern Lights."

Bailey stepped outside to shake his hand. "I'm Bailey, glad to meet you."

"I'll take a look at the weather predictions, and we'll set up a plan to go out Northern Lights viewing. Maybe we could meet for breakfast in the morning to discuss our search for the Northern Lights."

Bailey hesitated while her financial situation whirled through her head. Could she afford another meal on her limited budget?

"My treat." Alex saw the doubt on her face. He wasn't certain of her financial situation, but since she'd booked a two week stay, it was the least he could do. Especially, since he had no idea what he was going to put together for this Northern Lights tour she'd booked.

"Yes, that sounds good." Bailey felt relieved and she relaxed immediately.

"Great. Does eight work for you?"

"That's perfect," Bailey said offering him a bright smile. "I was just on my way up to the lodge for some dinner."

"I'm heading back up there myself. I can walk with you."

Bailey walked back into the cabin to get her purse and key. Alex waited outside.

They began walking up the hill to the lodge at a leisurely pace.

"This place is really beautiful. I'm not sure what I expected, but I have to admit, I'm not an outdoors-type gal, so this is a bit out of my comfort range. I've been working so much lately that I rarely get outdoors to do much of anything."

"I grew up here, so I know these woods like the back of my hand. This place is definitely in my comfort zone area."

Bailey laughed. "So, I'm in good hands?"

"You could say that." Alex grinned as they walked up the steps to the lodge. He held the door open for her, and she walked inside. "The restaurant is over there." He pointed to the door.

Bailey read the name on the glass door—Northern Delights. "I like the name."

"You'll have to taste the food first, and then let me know if you think it is a fitting name. If you like fish, I recommend the walleye. It's fresh caught and my mom is a great cook."

"I love walleye. I just might have to treat myself to a

walleye dinner tonight. It's been a long day. I feel like I've been driving all day, even though it was only five hours."

Alex held out his hand to shake hers. "It was nice to meet you, Bailey. I will see you here at eight tomorrow morning."

Bailey extended her hand to shake his and felt a tingling sensation flow through her body all the way to the pit of her stomach. "See you tomorrow," she said letting go of his hand. He dipped his head slightly and walked into the lodge office.

She opened the door to Northern Delights and was greeted by the hostess, who seated her at a table by the window overlooking the lake.

Her stomach was doing flip flops, just from shaking his hand. He was so good looking. How was she going to spend two weeks with him and not fall madly in love with him? She hadn't spent two weeks with any guy since her last boyfriend, which was three years ago. Her twenty-ninth birthday fell on July 25, which was in a couple of weeks, and she was still single. Her goal of having a successful business and being married by thirty was looking dimmer every day. Maybe the Northern Lights and Alex were exactly what she needed.

CHAPTER 4

"So, what do you think, Alex?" Renate asked.

"About what?"

"Our Northern Lights customer, Bailey?"

"She told me she's not an outdoors type person. Thanks a lot, Renate."

"Well, just make her feel safe and maybe you can convert her. It might just be she's never had the opportunity to try being an outdoors person."

"I guess I have my work cut out for me."

"It sounds like she's concerned about running into bears and wolves."

"She said that?"

"Well, she asked about them. I told her she was in good hands with my brother."

"Like I said, thanks a lot, sis."

"No problem."

"By the way, who was going to take her on the tour if I hadn't shown up?"

"Me?"

"You know you're darn lucky she's hot and seems likeable

or you *would* be taking her." He grabbed his jacket from the rack. "I'm taking some guys out fishing now. Hope you allotted some time for sleeping in my schedule." He walked out the door.

"Very funny!" she yelled after him.

He had his work cut out for him, that was for sure. Bailey was already out of her comfort zone and they weren't even in the woods yet. How could he make her feel safe? There was no predicting when or if bears or wolves would be in the area. He'd have to check to see if there'd been any sightings recently. Predicting when the Northern Lights would be visible wasn't up to him, either. He had no control over the weather. Cloudy skies or rain would prevent them from being seen. All he could do was pray for clear skies, so they'd stand a chance of observing them.

He was beginning to think he should've stayed in Minneapolis. If it weren't for the spark he'd felt when she'd put her hand in his, Renate might've been on Northern Lights duty. And if it weren't for the fact that Bailey's fit body was making his blood run hot, not to mention her long red hair and green eyes, Renate would've been doing the tour. As it stood right now, he was looking at it as a challenge in many more ways than one.

He wasn't sure if the fish would be biting tonight or if Bailey would bite at the chance to get to know him better, either, but he had two weeks to find out.

Bailey woke up to a beautiful sunrise and was looking forward to meeting Alex. She even put on extra makeup, including a second coat of mascara and dressed to entice. Nothing overly sexy, just more sexual allure than her usual attire provided.

She arrived promptly at eight to find him waiting for her. He'd obviously showered and shaved, not that she hadn't expected he would, but you never knew with the type of guys who liked the woods. She'd read somewhere that some of them didn't shower for days. Regardless, he looked darn good!

"Good morning, Bailey," he said greeting her with a handshake. She felt the tingling again.

"Good morning." She smiled up at Alex wondering what it would be like to be kissed by him.

He opened the door and led the way to a table with a view of the lake. The hostess trailed them quickly, handing them menus. He laid his down, since he probably knew what was on it because his family owned the resort. She opened hers and motioned yes to have her cup filled with fresh hot coffee.

"It's not Starbucks, but it's pretty good." Alex poured a couple drops of cream in his. "I recommend the French toast platter. My mom's recipe is the best I've ever had."

"Great, I'll try that," she said to the waitress. "With sausage and fruit."

"Me, too."

The waitress nodded, not asking any other questions since she probably knew his preferences.

"So, how'd you sleep?" Alex asked.

"Good, feeling refreshed and ready to go."

"Well, as I'm sure you know, viewing the Northern Lights is only an option on a clear night. And they have to be appearing on that night also, which is what makes it so difficult to predict. Tonight is supposed to be clear with occasional clouds and there is a chance for Northern Lights occurring. So, we can give it a shot tonight."

"Wow that's great! It's only my second night and we might see them?"

"Might is the key word here."

"I'm game."

"I'm assuming you brought warm clothes along as it can get cold at night?"

"Yes, I came prepared."

"How much equipment do you need to bring with for the photos?"

"Oh, not that much. Photography has advanced so much over the years. I'll only need my camera, tripod and a few other things that will fit in my backpack. I travel light."

"That's good, cuz I know a perfect spot to go that will require some climbing, but the view is phenomenal from up there."

The waitress set their plates in front of them. The French toast looked delicious and she couldn't wait to taste it.

Alex picked up the maple syrup to pour on his French toast. "We have our own Maple trees, so my mom makes this syrup for the lodge each year."

"Your mom sounds like quite the cook."

"She is. Cooking is her thing. We can't get her out of the kitchen. She's always in there either baking or cooking. My family members are all her testers for the new recipes she concocts."

Bailey poured maple syrup on her French toast and took a bite. "This is uniquely different and scrumptious. I'd love to meet her."

"Since you're going to be here for two weeks, I'm sure you will."

"So, tell me about your photography business."

"I've loved taking pictures since I was young, went to college for it, did a couple of internships in the industry and started my own photography business two years ago."

"So how is it going, having your own business?"

"Not as well as I thought it would. It's hard to make a name for yourself as a photographer unless you come up with some very unique photos that will draw interest and bring your name to the top of the lists, so people know who you are."

"So that's why you're here. Unique photos of the Northern Lights?"

"Exactly. If I can get some of my own great shots of them, I might be able to get out of the wedding photography business."

"Have something against weddings?"

"No, don't get me wrong, I don't have anything against weddings. It was paying the bills but didn't leave any time for my creative side that wanted to be out finding that perfect shot."

"Not doing weddings anymore?"

"No, at least not right now. My lease was up on my apartment, so I decided to move back home with my parents for a while to see if I can make some unique photos happen."

"I see. Your future depends on me getting you the right opportunity to take pictures of the Northern Lights?"

"Well, sort of. Otherwise, I'll have to be living at my parents' house longer and building my finances back up, so I can move out again. I've actually thought about giving up my dream and just getting a regular nine-to-five job in some office."

"You'd rather do that than weddings? Weddings are kind of fun, aren't they?"

"Not when you're working the whole time. And then there's a lot of work afterwards. Brides today are on tight budgets, so they don't want to spend very much. And nowadays everyone has a camera, so their friends get quite a few good shots and they don't have to pay for those pictures."

"Wow. Guess I don't know that much about the photography business."

"Sorry, don't mean to put any extra pressure on you. This

must be a great job, getting to do what you love—fishing and being outdoors."

"I have to say I do love fishing and being outdoors." Alex was truly intrigued by Bailey. He specifically worded his answer to avoid saying it was his job. He had women in the Cities always trying to get dates with him because he owned his own successful company. He never knew if they were really interested in him or the money he made. He'd done extremely well, but he wanted to find a woman who liked him for who he was. This was a perfect opportunity. He was intrigued by Bailey and if it went anywhere he'd know it was because she liked him as a Northern Lights tour guide not the owner of a multi-million-dollar company.

"If you want to give it a shot tonight, I'll meet you in the lodge lobby at eight thirty. Don't forget to dress warm."

"It's a date." Realizing how that just sounded, she added, "I don't think that came out right. I meant I'll see you then."

Alex laughed. "That's okay, I knew what you meant."

The waitress cleared their dishes and they both finished their coffee.

She gazed out the window at the lake. "I'm going to take a drive into town to pick up a few things. I'll see you tonight."

They both stood.

"Have a good day," Alex said and walked into the office as Bailey left the lodge.

CHAPTER 5

hank heavens the little town had a grocery store. Bailey picked up a few items for snacks—chips, pop, cereal, milk, luncheon meat, buns, cheese and a couple of frozen pizzas. She couldn't afford to eat out all the time on her limited budget, so these supplies would have to get her by for at least a week.

Next, she headed to Main Street to take a stroll past the shops. Looking was free even if she couldn't buy anything. The shops were filled with souvenir items from Northern Minnesota. Sweatshirts, pottery, clothing for the cold winter months, wooden carved items and, of course, jewelry for the women.

The one place she wanted to visit was the root beer lady's store. She walked into The Dorothy Molter Museum and paid the $7.00 entrance fee. From what she read at the museum, Dorothy was a strong, fiercely independent woman born in 1907 out East in Pennsylvania. Her mother died when she was seven, which sent her into an orphanage along with her five siblings until her father remarried and brought them to Chicago. She lived during the Women's Suffrage movement, WWI and WWII. Choosing education over marriage, she attended nursing school. After visiting Knife Lake in the Superior National Forest north of Ely in 1930, she came back often and helped run the Isle of Pines Resort, eventually becoming its owner from 1948 to 1986.

Wow, Bailey thought. What an incredible woman. If this woman could do all this back in the day when it wasn't even thought of for women to do anything but stay home and have babies, there wasn't any reason why she couldn't make her photography business work. She'd just have to try harder. And spend less. And live with her parents for a while.

In the museum shop, she purchased a bottle of Dorothy's homemade root beer. It was cold and refreshing. Bailey realized it made perfect sense that if Dorothy couldn't get supplies flown in after the president—Truman—ordered planes not to land on the lake, she had to come up with another plan. Which was making her own root beer. She was quite the entrepreneur. It tasted so refreshing, Bailey bought a six pack to take back.

Once she got back to her cabin, she decided to walk down to the boat dock and take some pictures of the lake. She noted the fishing boat was still out since the slip was empty. Mentally, she'd hoped to see Alex down at the lake.

At eight thirty, she walked up to the lodge ready to get her photos of the Northern Lights. The sun would be setting soon and after that they would go out into the woods and wait to see if they were visible. So far, the sky was almost cloudless, but that could change at any moment.

"So, it looks like you're ready to go," Alex said. "Let's get moving. I want to get up there before it gets dark. Just follow me."

Alex picked up his backpack and walked towards the woods with Bailey close behind him. They walked for about twenty minutes through the woods and up a hill leading out to a ledge overlooking the lake. He motioned for her to sit down.

"The view is breathtaking," Bailey said as she sat down. She opened her backpack and took out her camera and tripod. After setting it up, she took a seat next to Alex, where he silently watched her.

"Would I steer you wrong?"

She laughed. "Probably not, since it's your job."

Unfortunately, as the sun set the clouds rolled in, which meant tonight was not the night.

"We can stay a little bit longer and see if the clouds move out, if you'd like."

"Sure."

"So, what would you like to talk about?" Alex stared into her eyes.

"The Northern Lights," Bailey offered.

"Do you want to know what causes them?"

Bailey nodded yes.

"Well, it has to do with charged electrons and protons, ionization, and the earth's magnetic fields. Typically, in this area they are greenish colors."

"Okay, now when do you think they will be appearing?"

"The clouds are getting heavier, so I'd say not tonight. We should head back."

Bailey put her equipment and camera away. Alex was waiting and when he saw she was ready, he began the walk back down to the resort. She followed quietly so as to not attract any critters.

Alex walked her to the door of her cabin. "Oh, I almost forgot. Renate wanted me to tell you breakfast and lunch are included with your tour package. It's a new tour and she forgot to list it on the receipt she sent you."

"Really? That's great news. It'll certainly help me out."

"With that taken care of, would you care to join me for breakfast in the morning?"

"I'd love to."

"Same time okay for you?"

"Sounds good."

She opened the door to the cabin and went inside as Alex walked up to his family's cabin.

Alex saw his mom and dad sitting in the great room watching television along with Renate.

"So, how'd it go?" Renate probed.

"As I'm sure you noticed, the clouds rolled in thick and heavy. Didn't want to spend the whole night waiting for the unlikely chance they would move out."

"Good call, son," his dad offered.

"Did you get along okay?" his mom asked.

"Yes, we got along fine. She's a nice lady. And by the way, I told her breakfast and dinner were included with her tour package."

"Well, I suppose we can do that since you obviously thought we should. Just wondering though, why you decided to do that?" Renate asked.

"She spent probably all the savings she had left to book this tour, so she could take pictures of the Northern Lights. Actually, she moved back in with her parents and is thinking about giving up her photography business if this doesn't pan out."

"Oh. We always have plenty of food, so it's not a problem as far as I'm concerned," his mom said.

"Great. I'm going to bed." Alex walked upstairs to his room. He just might have to take a cold shower first, though. This had been one of the toughest nights he'd ever spent with a woman. He'd just spent the evening with someone who he was immensely attracted to, but since she was a customer at the resort, he couldn't show his interest and had to be a perfect gentleman. He was pretty sure he couldn't do it for two weeks.

CHAPTER 6

*T*he sun was shining brightly through the windows of her bedroom when she woke up. She'd struggled to fall asleep, because she kept thinking about Alex. Strong, handsome, Alex. Someone who she could easily fall for, so she'd definitely need to play it cool.

Alex was waiting in the lobby. "This way." He led the way to the same booth they'd shared the morning before. The coffee pot was on the table waiting for them. She reached for the pot and poured them both a cup.

"Is there a breakfast special today? I thought I saw something on the sign when we came in."

"Today, Mom is making the thin style Swedish pancakes with eggs and bacon. They're great!"

"I love them. Sounds good to me."

He motioned to the waitress and held up two fingers, which she assumed meant they each wanted the special. They discussed the weather and how the night tour had gone, and soon the waitress set their breakfast specials in front of them. It looked delicious.

"My morning is open today, so I was wondering how you felt about fishing?" Alex flashed her a bright smile.

"I like fishing. But... Do you bait hooks?" Bailey gave him her damsel in distress look.

"I can bait your hook for you, if that's what you're asking."

"I usually am good at catching fish, but I don't bait my hook or take the fish off the hook."

Alex laughed. "Okay, let's see who catches the most fish. Mostly what is caught on this lake is walleye. How about you meet me down at the dock in an hour?"

"I'll be there." They walked out of the lodge together. Alex went down to the boat house, and Bailey went to her cabin to put on her swimsuit under a pair of shorts and tank top. It was already in the low seventies and promised to reach eighty at least. It would be a hot one, for sure.

Bailey opted to bring a shirt along and wear just the swimsuit top and shorts. As she approached the dock, she saw Alex on the speedboat already wearing swim trunks and no shirt. Wow, he must work out. She was having second thoughts about going fishing at this point. He was such a nice guy and he had a six pack! Who'd of thought that?

She reached for his extended hand and stepped into the boat.

"Take a seat. I'm glad you wore your swimsuit. It's going to be a hot one." He started the engine and they glided across the smooth water. "I know the perfect spot."

The shoreline only had a few cabins tucked in here and there, otherwise it was mostly secluded. The lake was larger than she'd anticipated, but before she knew it the motor stopped, and he dropped the anchor. He proceeded to get the fishing rods ready and baited the hooks, before handing one to her.

"Thanks," she said and took the rod. She waited until he dropped his line in the water and then did the same. They were using bobbers, which was what she was used to and preferred.

"Okay, any bets on who catches the first fish?"

"I don't want to brag, but I usually do," she stated.

"What are we betting?" Alex grinned. If he had it his way he would choose a kiss for his prize, but that wouldn't be happening.

"A dollar?" Bailey offered. Just then she watched her bobber go under and wished she said something more like twenty dollars instead. She set the hook, just the way her father taught her and began reeling in the fish.

Alex grabbed the net and scooped a walleye onto the boat. "Wow, I'm impressed, probably a three pounder." He dropped the net on the floor to spin around and grab his rod as he saw his bobber go under. Quickly he set the hook and pulled in a one pounder he grabbed with his hand.

"I think mine is bigger," Bailey pointed out while Alex took both fish off the hooks and dropped them into the holding tank, then baited both hooks again.

"Yes, it is, and I owe you a dollar. So, tell me, do you by any chance clean fish?"

"Definitely not. They're slimy and then there are the scales. Yuk!"

"Exactly what I thought you'd say." Alex laughed.

"I do cook them, if that's any help."

"Excellent. That is an important part—along with eating them!"

Bailey burst out laughing as they dropped their lines in the water again. Not long after, they both caught another fish and another fish and another fish. Soon they'd reached their limit.

"I guess you sure do know the right spot for fishing."

"I know I do, at least I think I do, but this is certainly a good catch today." Alex essentially just wanted to be the one to catch her. He was actually starting to like her. She was fun and easy to be around. Definitely, not a pain in the butt, like he'd expected. No, she was just a real down to earth person trying to make her way in this crazy world by taking pictures.

"When we get back, I'd like to get a few photos of the fish we caught."

"Definitely. Would you like a tour of the lake before we go back?"

"I'd love it." Bailey sat down and took in the beautiful scenery of northern Minnesota as they skirted the shoreline.

After they'd docked the boat, she ran up to her cabin to get her camera. Alex had her big fish ready on a hook, so she could get a good shot.

"How about I take one of you holding it?" he asked.

"That's a great idea." Bailey handed him the camera and picked up the largest fish she'd caught and smiled for the photo.

"I'm going to get these cleaned and take the filets up to my mom in the kitchen. If it's okay with you, I'll have her cook us a couple filets for dinner? There is nothing like eating them when they are fresh caught."

"Excellent idea. What time should I come up for dinner?"

"See you up at the lodge at six," Alex said as he picked up the bucket of fish and headed to the fish cleaning shack.

Bailey showered and met Alex for dinner at the lodge. This time he was already seated at their table waiting and waved when he saw her in the doorway. She took a seat at the table and couldn't help looking out the window at the calm lake.

"Mom was happy to grill the filets for us. She likes to try different things, so she is making us an assortment of grilled, blackened and fried. I wasn't sure what you preferred so I thought this would hopefully offer one you liked."

The waitress brought out salads for each of them and a basket of fresh baked rolls.

"Oh, I like my fish just about any way you can make it, so all of those will work."

"So, do you like all kinds of fish, too?"

"Pretty much."

"Definitely, my kind of gal." Alex loved watching her face brighten with a smile. And knowing it was meant for him made him feel pretty darn good.

"What's the latest weather forecast for tomorrow?" Bailey asked.

"I think it's supposed to rain the next couple of days, but Friday is supposed to be sunny and clear skies all evening. I think that's our best bet on seeing the Northern Lights."

"Okay. So, what do you do up here at the resort when it rains?"

"Well, a little rain never hurt anyone."

"I guess there is always going shopping in town. Well most likely not shopping but looking anyway."

"I heard you were concerned about bears and wolves around here." Alex raised his eye brow and grinned at her.

"I'm assuming Renate mentioned it? Well, they are dangerous, aren't they?"

"Only if they are starving or antagonized. Otherwise they pretty much steer away from any human contact."

"Still...they scare the crap out of me."

"There is the International Wolf Center and the North American Bear Center, both are located in Ely. You can see live animals and learn about them, too, which might make them less scary. If you'd like I can go into town with you tomorrow and we can check them out?"

"Are you sure? I don't want to take you away from your job at the resort."

"Since I'm your tour guide for the Northern Lights and

we won't be able to go in the rain, I can certainly be your tour guide for the wolves and bears. Who knows, you might even get some great photo shots while we're there."

"Well, if you put it that way, I did come up here to take pictures. Sure, why not. It should be a safe environment."

The waitress appeared with their dinner—walleye filets cooked three different ways, oven browned potatoes and a vegetable medley.

"This looks heavenly," Bailey said as she and Alex began enjoying their catch for the day.

"My mom wanted to be sure we have some of her 'from-scratch' Chocolate Buttermilk Cake for dessert. It's one of my favorites." Alex didn't mention his mom made it especially for him since he was up at the lodge this month.

"I'll never pass up anything chocolate, especially home-made! I'm in."

The waitress brought out the chocolate cake after they'd finished eating.

"This is what is referred to as 'chocolate to die for.' Tell your mother I loved it!"

After dinner, Alex walked Bailey back to her cabin. It almost felt like she'd been on a date, but she hadn't. So that meant a good night kiss was out of the question.

"Hope you had a good day. You got some pictures of fish, anyway," Alex joked. "And tomorrow we'll get you some of wolves and bears."

"Not exactly what I came up here for, but any pictures are better than no pictures."

"Breakfast then? Same time? And then your tour of Ely's bears and wolves?"

"Sounds good," Bailey said. She unlocked her cabin door and waved good bye to Alex as he walked away back up to his family's cabin.

She closed the door behind her and leaned back against it.

Wow! That was the best day and dinner date—that wasn't a date—that she'd had in a very long time. Alex was one of those really nice guys, in fact she couldn't fault him on anything, so far. And now she got to spend the whole day tomorrow with him, too. Life was good.

CHAPTER 7

*a*fter breakfast, Alex pulled his black Chevy Suburban up to the lodge to pick her up. It was a short ride into town and they parked at the North American Bear Center first. There was an hour-long audio tour with headsets that they took first to learn all about the bears, their habitats and daily patterns. Then they headed out back to the viewing area, which consisted of an inside glassed-in area or outside viewing deck above the living area of the bears.

"Inside or outside?" Alex asked.

"Outside. Then maybe I can get some photos." Bailey took her camera out and zipped up her bag.

"I can hold that for you," Alex offered.

"Thanks." Bailey handed him her bag, so she could concentrate on the photo shots.

Luckily there was a break in the clouds and the sun shone brightly. Bailey walked back and forth on the balcony, clicking away, picture after picture. When she felt she'd have enough to choose from, she stopped.

"Got enough, I take it?"

"Might have some good ones in all those."

It was afternoon when they left and headed to The International Wolf Center. Everything you ever wanted to know about wolves could be found at this center. The exhibits contained a wealth of knowledge. They also participated in the audio tour to get the max out of the displays. Once they arrived at the live wolf area, Bailey took out her camera. She stepped out to the outside viewing area and began clicking away.

Alex stood observing Bailey, her camera, and the wolves. The way she lovingly held the camera, moving this way and that way until she had the perfect shot, moved him. He could understand now why she didn't want to give up her photography. It was almost like it was a part of her, as she moved in for the shot.

He was determined to make sure she got her pictures of the Northern Lights. Each time he'd witnessed them throughout the years, he couldn't believe his eyes. There just weren't any words to describe the overwhelming feeling the Northern Lights created while watching them.

He wanted Bailey to have that opportunity. He'd even found an app for his phone that could pinpoint his location and let him know when they would be visible. He hoped this worked, cuz staying up all night each night was the only other option. Or just lucking out by being out there on the right night was the best one, but it was simply a craps shoot at best.

"So, what do you think, get some good ones?" Alex said as he handed her the bag and she put the camera away.

"Hope so. Took a lot anyway," she answered.

"It's about six already. There is a new restaurant down the road from here that recently opened and typically has live music. I've been meaning to check it out, care to give it a try? My treat."

Bailey couldn't believe she almost declined his offer. She

could maybe afford to have a drink, but dinner? Probably not. And since dinner was included, she should just eat at the resort. But she really enjoyed spending time with him, so maybe she could take him up on it? Was it a date then?

"It sounds like fun, but you don't have to take me, and you don't have to pay for me. I sort of feel like I'm imposing on you. Like maybe there is someone else you'd like to take or should be taking there?"

"Okay, let's try this again. I'm not dating anyone. I like you, Bailey. Would you like to go to dinner with me?"

"Like a real date?" Bailey couldn't believe her ears.

"Yes. And I'm old fashioned. If I take someone on a date, I pay."

"Well then, I'd love to." Her face lit up and she gave him that beautiful smile of hers. A real date. It had been a long time.

"Although, I'm assuming you aren't, I do have to ask, are you dating anyone?"

"No."

The restaurant was a short drive out of town. They pulled up at the Rockwood Bar and Grill, which ended up being the restaurant she'd wanted to check out. How perfect. The parking lot was beginning to fill up, which usually meant it was a good place to eat.

Alex asked for a table on the patio since the weather had cleared up. Heck, what do the weathermen know? The sun was shining, and the temp was about eighty.

"Can I get you something to drink?" the waiter asked.

"What do you suggest?" Alex asked.

"Our Roknar Smash is quite popular."

"Sound okay, Bailey?" Alex asked.

"Sure. I'm game to try it."

Minutes later they were sipping on their drinks while

looking over the menu. The waiter returned to take their order.

"I'll try the smoked pork chop. The root beer glaze sounds intriguing," Bailey answered.

"I'm going to go with the stuffed meatloaf."

"Care to add soup or salad? May I recommend the blueberry salad, it's one of our specialties?" the waiter asked.

"Sure, we'll give it a try," Alex said as Bailey nodded.

They watched as the band finished setting up and began playing smooth jazz music. Opposite of the area where the band was, a beautiful waterfall flowed gently. The ambiance on the patio was perfect. Perfect for a couple in love.

Their salads arrived proving to be unique but very delicious. They sipped their drinks while they ate and savored the smooth music filling the air.

The entrees appeared soon after they finished their salads. The aromas wafting from the plates were tempting her taste buds for their turn. This unique, one-of-a-kind restaurant out in the middle of nowhere could rival any of the downtown Minneapolis restaurants.

"This is delightful," Bailey stated savoring the flavors abounding in her mouth.

"Mine, too. Would you like to taste mine?" he asked.

He was behaving like they were a couple. She'd never tasted food off someone's plate who she'd newly started dating, that usually took a while. His meatloaf looked good, though. "Sure. Do you want to taste mine?" Bailey cut off a piece of her pork chop and set it on his plate and he did the same.

"They must have a superb chef here. I'd definitely come back. Don't get me wrong, I love my mom's cooking. Heck, I grew up with it and it is definitely a comfort food style. But I enjoy this new age fine dining cuisine, immensely too."

"I have to agree," Bailey said.

After dinner, they listened a bit longer to the band before heading back to the resort. He pulled up in front of her cabin and got out to open her door.

"I had a nice time, Alex. Thank you," Bailey said.

"Me, too. Thanks for joining me." Alex looked into her eyes and at her lips. He wanted to kiss her, but it wouldn't be appropriate, so he slowly backed away. "See you at breakfast tomorrow." He got in his SUV and drove up to his family's cabin.

CHAPTER 8

*B*ailey met Alex for breakfast and they decided to wait one more day, since it was raining again.

"I need to help my dad with some repairs on the boat house. Dinner at six?" he asked.

"See you then," Bailey said and went back to her cabin to work on her photos.

It was still completely cloudy with on and off showers when she walked up to the lodge for dinner. She'd worked all afternoon on her photos and was famished. Her steps quickened, and she realized it was Alex she was eager to see.

He was waiting at their usual table, as she walked into the restaurant and took a seat across from him.

"Hi, how was your afternoon?" Alex asked.

"Good. I think I got some good shots. Bears, wolves and fish." She laughed. "Not exactly what I came here for, but they're not bad at all."

"We're still working on those coveted Northern Lights shots," he said.

"The boat house repaired?"

"Yes, my dad is happy."

"I ordered us the special—fried chicken and mashed potatoes. Does that sound okay to you?"

"I like chicken. Sounds good."

After dinner, he walked her back to her cabin. It was just starting to sprinkle again.

"I have an early morning fishing excursion tomorrow and one in the afternoon, so I won't be able to meet you for breakfast or dinner. It's supposed to clear up though, so I think we can try tomorrow evening about nine to get you those pictures of the Northern Lights," Alex said.

"Okay, I'm looking forward to it. See you tomorrow night at nine." Bailey waved as he walked away, but she was disappointed to say the least. She'd enjoyed his company and looked forward to their meals together.

In the morning, she made her way up to the lodge about nine for breakfast. The waitress seated her at the usual table. She could see the dock from the window and noticed the empty boat slip. It was a bright sunny morning and the temperature would be rising to eighty. This would be the perfect opportunity to sit down at the lake and get a little sun. She had brought along a romance novel just in case she found some time to read.

That's where she was, in her bikini at the beach, when the boat came back with Alex and the four guys he'd taken out fishing. Thankfully, she was wearing her sunglasses, so he couldn't tell she was staring at his tanned bare chest.

After everyone disembarked from the boat to go on their way, he walked over to her.

"Hi," he said.

Bailey noticed his appreciative gaze slide up and down her body, so she sat up and tilted her glasses down to look over the tops of them. "Hi. How was the fishing?"

"We didn't reach the limits, but everyone caught a couple,

so they were happy. Glad to see you got a chance to enjoy the beach."

"Me, too. Haven't had a chance to read a book for a long time. I'm enjoying it."

"Well, need to get these fish cleaned. See you tonight."

Bailey made her way back to her cabin about four. She hadn't noticed the boat leaving again, so she must've fallen asleep. After a quick shower, she went to the lodge to eat dinner. Eating alone was the one thing she especially hated about being single.

The evening flew by. She loaded up her backpack, put some warm clothing on since the temperature was dropping as sunset approached, and walked up to the lodge. It was a nice evening, so she sat down on the front steps to wait for Alex.

A few minutes later, he was standing in front of her. "Ready?" he asked.

"Sure am," she said standing up.

"Let's do this," he said smiling. "I'm feeling lucky. I think we're going to see the Northern Lights tonight."

"Lead on," she said, following Alex.

Once they got to the ledge, she set up her camera and took a seat next to Alex. It was so much darker up north than in the cities, but it allowed the lights from the stars to shine brighter.

"I'm assuming since you grew up here, you've seen the Northern Lights before?" Bailey asked.

"Yes, quite a few times. They are beautiful. I take it you've *never* seen them?"

"Living in the Twin Cities my whole life, made it pretty much impossible." She got up to check her tripod and camera to make sure they were set up correctly. The timer mechanism would come in handy tonight. She didn't want anything to go wrong. These pictures meant everything to her.

She sat back down to wait.

"Relax. Usually, they don't show up until midnight. So what would you like to talk about?"

"Did you go to college?" she asked.

"Yes, the University of Minnesota in Minneapolis where I earned a degree in business."

"Oh, so you've spent time in Minneapolis, then."

"A few years, anyway."

"I think I mentioned before that I attended the Minneapolis College of Art and Design."

"Yes, you did. You seem nervous."

"I've wanted to see the Northern Lights for a few years now. I can't believe it might happen tonight."

They both were staring into the sky when streaks of green began appearing. Soon almost the whole sky was green with small streaks of pink. Bailey jumped up and switched the camera on. It would take delayed shots to capture the intense colors. She stood back and stared at the sky and then pulled another camera out of her bag to use to take pictures.

"This is incredible! Totally worth the wait and the money. I've never seen anything like this in my entire life. Oh my, look over there," she said putting the smaller camera in her pocket and walking over towards the other side of the ledge where her camera on the tripod was positioned.

Alex walked over to stand beside her and gaze into the sky at the phenomenon they were witnessing together. Standing behind her, he put his arm around her waist and pulled her back into his chest, partly because he was worried she was too close to the edge, but partly because it was something he'd wanted to do since he'd met her.

Bailey turned around and was facing him, now. "This is a once in a lifetime experience for me. Thank you so much." Overwhelmed with the beauty they were witnessing, she reached up and kissed him. It felt so good. She felt his arms tighten and pull her close to his chest and realized he was kissing her back. If this was wrong she could always say she was sorry, later. Even if she didn't feel one ounce of sorry.

Alex ended the kiss and turned her back around to face the Northern Lights, moving them both over away from the ledge and the camera. "You're missing the show," he said but kept his arms around her. He continued to embrace her until the lights began fading, about an hour later.

Neither said anything about the kiss as she packed up her camera equipment. He led the way back and she followed in silence. At her cabin, she opened the door as he stood watching and waiting to see what she was going say.

"I'm tired and it's late. Will you be at breakfast?" she asked.

Alex smiled. "Wouldn't miss it."

"Thanks so much for tonight." She walked into the cabin and closed the door.

The next morning, she got up early to look at her pictures. She had managed to get numerous good shots. This could be her big break! There were even a few of the kiss. She hadn't intended for that to happen at all. She was just so overwhelmed by the incredible light show they were witnessing, she'd kissed him. Fortunately, he kissed her back, or she would be totally embarrassed now.

Alex was already seated at the table waiting for her when she walked into the restaurant. He smiled at her as she approached the table.

"How'd you sleep last night," he asked as she sat down.

"Not the best. I think I had too much excitement for one night."

"It was a good night. I ordered the breakfast special for us. It's Belgian waffles with fresh strawberries today."

"Sounds delicious." Bailey was having a hard time looking

into his bright blue eyes this morning. She didn't think she would, but she felt embarrassed.

"Did you get a chance to look at the photos? Any good ones?"

"There are quite a few excellent shots. I will be forever grateful to you for taking me out to the ledge. It was the perfect place to take photos."

The waitress brought out their food and it looked scrumptious. She didn't realize how hungry she was as she relished her first bite.

After breakfast, Alex walked Bailey back to her cabin.

"What's the plan for today? Looking at your photos?" he asked.

"Actually, I'm going to head back to the Twin Cities today. I should have all the photos I need and I'm excited to start working on them, so I can get ready for the Minneapolis Art Fair the first weekend in August on Nicollet Island."

"You can't stay a few more days? You're booked for two weeks."

"I know but I need to get back."

"Can I call you?" Alex asked.

"I'd like that." Bailey wanted to throw her arms around his neck and kiss him so hard he'd surely want to call her. She didn't have any idea how he felt though, so it wasn't going to happen.

"I do need your number to call you," Alex said.

"Of course," she reached into her purse and pulled out her business card and handed it to him.

"Sure I can't change your mind?"

Bailey shook her head. She wished she could tell him she'd probably already fallen madly in love him, but that wasn't happening, either.

"I will call you. Good luck with the Northern Lights

photos. Don't forget me." Alex gave her his sexy grin and walked back to the lodge.

Bailey loaded her car, then stopped up at the lodge to turn in her key. The bill was prepaid, so she was all set. Thankfully, neither Renate nor Alex were at the counter. Within minutes, she was on the road back home. She was sure she'd just made a huge mistake by leaving, but Alex needed to make the first move and call her. The last week had been one of the best weeks she'd ever had.

*a*lex slammed the door to the office behind him. "She left." He plopped down in the chair facing Renate's desk.

"What did you do?" she asked.

"What did I do? It was her. She kissed me, so I kissed her back."

"Oh, I see. The Northern Lights were out last night, right?"

"Yes, she got her photos."

"She kissed you on the ledge after seeing them?"

"Exactly."

"What did you do after that? Did you talk to her about it? Tell her how you felt?"

"No. And she didn't really give me a chance this morning. Just said she got the photos and was leaving."

"Did you get her phone number?"

"Yes."

"Thank heavens! At least you did one thing right. Wait a few days and call her."

"Dating advice from my sister?"

"I take it you really like her."

"Yes, I liked her. She's beautiful, smart and a real person. I actually think she liked me for me."

"Then you better not let her get away. Hopefully she won't be mad when she finds out you're some rich business owner instead of a tour guide."

"Exactly. Tell Dad, I'm leaving. I need to get back to Minneapolis."

Instead of calling, he sent Bailey a text saying he was looking forward to seeing her and her photos at the Minneapolis Art Fair.

That day, he arrived at Nicollet Island about four. The event was scheduled to end at five, so he thought it would be winding down about then and maybe she could use some help taking down her booth. As he approached, he saw photos hung on the outside of her tent. There in front of his eyes was a photo of the Northern Lights with a shadow of a couple kissing in the foreground. It was incredible. He'd never seen anything like it. She'd captured the beauty of the lights with the sensuality of a couple in love. It was right in front of his eyes on the canvas. It was them—Bailey and him. He looked at the price tag. She was asking one thousand dollars for the twenty by ten canvas photo print.

He walked around and into the tent. There she was, as beautiful as he remembered. She looked up and saw him.

"You came," she stated, staring at him.

"I told you I would," he said as he closed the gap between them and stopped right in front of her. The chemistry between them was electrifying. "I want to buy the photo of us kissing. Put a sold sign on it, and then I need to talk to you. Privately."

He noticed an older woman who must've been helping her come back into the tent.

"I'll be right back," she said to the woman and led him out of the tent. She kept walking toward the river where they could be alone. She stopped and waited for him to talk first.

"I need to tell you something and I'm not quite sure where to begin, but this might be a good place to start." He handed her his business card.

She took the card, read his name and then his title which was CEO of Below Zero Clothing. That name was on the cold weather clothes her mom bought for her before she went up to Ely. "What does this mean?"

"That's my company. I started it out of college and it's now worth millions. I live in Minnetonka. I'm sorry I didn't tell you."

"You're a millionaire? That's a lot to take in. But why are you telling me this?"

"I'm falling in love with you. I hope you at least like me a little?"

"Probably more than a little." She smiled.

"I didn't tell you because I wanted you to like me for me and not my money."

"I do like the Alex I met in Ely. Is he the same guy as you are, Mr. CEO?"

"Most definitely. Can I kiss you now?"

"I've been wondering what you've been waiting for."

She didn't have to say any more. He'd been waiting for this moment since the day she'd left Ely. He took her in his arms and when his lips met hers, he kissed her.

She'd fallen in love with Alex and thankfully he was falling in love with her. What more could she ask for?

Bailey never imagined a kiss under the Northern Lights could have the power to change her life forever and make all her dreams come true.

RECIPE

CHOCOLATE BUTTERMILK CAKE WITH
FROSTING

Ingredients

- 1 cup butter
- 1/3 cup unsweetened cocoa
- 1 cup water
- 1/2 cup buttermilk
- 2 large eggs
- 1 teaspoon baking soda
- 1 teaspoon vanilla
- 2 cups sugar
- 2 cups all-purpose flour
- 1/4 teaspoon salt

Chocolate-Buttermilk Frosting

- 1 cup butter
- 1/4 cup unsweetened cocoa
- 1/3 cup buttermilk
- 2 cups confectioners' sugar
- 1 teaspoon vanilla

- 1/2 cup toasted pecans (optional)

Instructions

- Preheat oven to 350 degrees and grease a 9X13-inch pan.
- In small bowl melt butter in microwave. Add cocoa and hot water stirring until smooth.
- Using an electric mixer, beat buttermilk, eggs, baking soda, and vanilla until smooth in large bowl. Gradually add melted butter mixture.
- Add sugar, flour and salt to buttermilk mixture and beat until blended.
- Pour batter into prepared pan. Bake for 30 to 35 minutes, or until set in the middle.

- To make frosting, combine melted butter, cocoa, and buttermilk in a medium bowl. Stir constantly, until mixture is smooth. Add in confectioners' sugar, vanilla, and pecans.
- Pour over cake while cake is still warm. Let frosting cool and set before slicing.

ABOUT THE AUTHOR

ROSE MARIE MEUWISSEN

Rose Marie Meuwissen, a first-generation Norwegian American born and raised in Minnesota, always tries to incorporate her Norwegian heritage into her writing. After receiving a BA in Marketing from Concordia University, a Masters in Creative Writing from Hamline University soon followed. Minnesota is still where she calls home.

She has traveled around the world, including Scandinavia, but still has many places to see, enjoys attending Scandinavian events, writing conferences and is usually busy writing Minnesota Lakes Contemporary Romances, Viking Time Travel Romances or Norwegian Traditions Children's Books.

Visit her at www.rosemariemeuwissen.com or www.realnorwegianseatlutefisk.com.

NOVELS

- *Taking Chances*—a contemporary romance novel set in Minnesota and Arizona.
- *Married by Saturday*—a contemporary romance novel set in Minnesota and Montana.
- *Looking for Mr. Right*—a contemporary internet dating romance novel set on Prior Lake in Minnesota—*Coming soon!*

NOVELLAS

- *Annika—A Christmas Romance*—a contemporary romance set in Minnesota with a Nordic theme during the Christmas Holidays.
- *Skol! Viking Blonde Ale*—a contemporary romance set in Minnesota at an Autumn festival complete with a fortune teller, ale and Vikings!
- *Choosing to Live*—a Norwegian woman's journey during WWII to survive the Nazi Occupation of Norway—*Coming soon!*

MINNESOTA LAKES ROMANCE NOVELETTES

- *A Kiss Under the Northern Lights*—a Summer romance set in Ely, Minnesota on Big Lake.
- *Dancing in the Moonlight*—a Summer romance set in Malmo, Minnesota on Mille Lacs Lake.
- *Hot Summer Nights*—a Summer romance set in Prior Lake, Minnesota on Prior Lake.
- *Railroad Ties*—an Autumn romance set in Two Harbors, Minnesota on Lake Superior.
- *Blizzard of Love*—a Winter romance set in Lutsen, Minnesota on Lake Superior.
- *Nor-Way to Love*—a Spring romance set in Minneapolis, Minnesota on Lake Harriet.
- *Old Yule Log Fires*—a Christmas romance set in Excelsior, Minnesota on Lake Minnetonka.
- *A Date for Valentine's Day*—a Valentine romance set in Minnetonka Beach, Minnesota at the Lafayette Country Club on Lake Minnetonka.
- *Dance of Love*—a Fall Festival romance set at the Renaissance Fair in Shakopee, Minnesota.

CHILDREN'S BOOKS—REAL NORWEGIAN'S SERIES

- ***Real Norwegians Eat Lutefisk***—a Children's book about the tradition of Lutefisk presented in both English and Norwegian.
- ***Real Norwegians Eat Rømmegrøt***—the second Children's book in the series about the tradition of Rømmegrøt presented in both English and Norwegian.
- ***Real Norwegians Eat Lefse***—the third Children's book in the series about the tradition of Lefse presented in both English and Norwegian.
- ***Real Norwegians Eat Krumkake***—the fourth Children's book in the series about the tradition of Krumkake presented in both English and Norwegian—***Coming next!***

MICRO-MINI NOVELETTE—COMING SOON!

- ***Christmas Notes***—a collection of Christmas prose poems to warm the heart during the Christmas season.

CONTINUE READING FOR A
PREVIEW OF:

SKOL! VIKING BLONDE ALE

Fortunes, Love & Fate Series

By

Rose Marie Meuwissen

SKOL! VIKING BLONDE ALE-COVER

SKOL! VIKING BLONDE ALE—
COPYRIGHT

FORTUNES, LOVE & FATE SERIES

Print Edition
Copyright 2020 by Rose Marie Meuwissen

ISBN 978-0-9903788-3-9

Published in the United States of America
Nordic Publishing LLC
Cover Design by Raine English

SKOL! VIKING BLONDE ALE—INTRO

FORTUNES, LOVE & FATE SERIES

Inga was living the dream, planning events for her own company, Unique Events, but she still hadn't found a guy who could be 'The One' for her. She never would've believed a fortune from a gypsy fortune teller promising her a 'love that surpasses time' could come true.

Erik moved from Norway to Minnesota to expand his Nordic Brewing company in the U. S. He'd promised himself to devote all his time to the business, but how was he to know that an unknown force of fate would introduce him to a woman he couldn't walk away from?

Their attraction could not be denied because ultimately, they were destined to be together. But could the Atlantic Ocean keep them apart? Would that even be possible if they were truly soul mates?

INGA'S FORTUNE

Someone from your past will reappear in your life.
Your true soul mate.
With him, you will experience a love that surpasses time.

PROLOGUE

James J. Hill Days in Wayzata
on Lake Minnetonka

September

*I*nga pulled into the back-parking lot of Main Street Books at six. She couldn't believe it wasn't later. Friday night rush hour traffic on the 494 Freeway was bumper to bumper all the way from Eden Prairie to Wayzata. The weather was still holding its summer like temps and true Minnesotans would never pass up a beautiful autumn weekend to go up North to their cabins one last time before winter arrived. Today was the James J. Hill Days celebration in Wayzata and the main street was packed with people as she made her way into the book store to find her *Romancing the Lakes of Minnesota* book club. This month instead of their regular meeting, they planned to enjoy walking around and checking out the celebration. Probably was a good call, she thought, since it would've been difficult to hold their meeting in the crowded book store and the activity outside would've been immensely distracting.

"Am I the last one to arrive?" Inga asked as she approached the book club group standing in front of the latest arrival shelf where the romance section was located.

"Bet the traffic was awful," Nora stated.

"Ready, to brave the crowds?" Katie asked.

"I'm hungry and thirsty, let's go!" Violet said.

Inga nodded in agreement and followed the group out the door to Main Street. They made their way down the street stopping at booths to look at the novelties for sale until finally, they stopped at the end of the street where the most unusual trailer was parked. The sign above the open door read, 'Fortune Teller'. It appeared to be Vintage, but these days they could make anything look old, even if it was new. Although, she had to admit, she'd never seen anything like it before, even though she'd been to many events. After all, she was an event planner. Intrigued was putting it mildly. Unfortunately, there was no stopping her curiosity. So, she entered the trailer.

"Come in, please," a very thickly accented voice beckoned from inside the trailer.

"Hello." Inga ducked and stepped into the trailer, taking in all the antiques and draped surroundings.

"Take a seat," the lady in gypsy like garb directed. "Let me see what your life has in store for you."

Inga didn't believe in fortune telling, at least she didn't think she did, but what could it possibly hurt to oblige the lady. It might be worth a laugh later, so she sat down on the partially pulled out chair at the table.

The fortune teller took the seat across from Inga and reached for her hand.

Slowly, Inga extended her hand. When their hands

touched, Inga felt a strange sensation flow through her entire body, almost like a spark of electricity. It only lasted a few seconds and then was gone. She had no idea what it was or what caused it, but she finally relaxed.

The woman's face seemed deep in thought and completely fixated on her hand. "You are a very special lady. Very strong and independent. I see happiness in your future."

"Do you see a man?" Inga wasn't sure why'd she'd asked that particular question.

"Yes." The woman continued staring at her hand. "A very handsome man."

"Well, there certainly are enough good-looking men around. What I need is one that is interested in me long enough to stick around for a while."

"You have not met '*The One*' yet."

"When? When will it happen? I'm getting really tired of waiting around for him."

"Soon."

"So, is that my fortune?"

"No." The woman hesitated, then picked up a piece of paper and wrote a few lines down on it. She handed it to Inga. "This is your fortune: *Someone from your past will reappear in your life. Your true soul mate. With him, you will experience a love that surpasses time.*"

"Great. But I'm sorry, I don't believe in magic."

"That's okay you don't have to believe. It will happen anyway."

Their eyes locked for a moment.

Inga got up to leave. "How much do I owe you?" Inga asked.

"For you, no charge. I've been waiting for you."

"I don't understand."

The fortune teller waived her hand in a shooing motion, indicating Inga was done and should leave.

As Inga stepped out of the trailer, Katie rushed up the steps. "My turn."

"So, what do you think? Is the Fortune Teller legit?" Violet asked.

"What kind of a question is that? Of course, it's not real. No one can tell another person what will happen in their future," Stephanie said.

"Care to share?" Nora asked.

Inga handed the piece of paper to Violet, who in turn handed it to Stephanie, who in turn handed it to Gwen and lastly to Nora.

"At least it's a good fortune. Let's hope it comes true," Stephanie said.

"Come on, you're not buying into this stuff, are you?" Inga shook her head.

Minutes later, Katie came down the trailer's steps, paper in hand grinning from ear to ear.

Violet practically ran to the steps to be next.

Each romance book club member shared their fortune while the next one took their turn. Being romantics at heart, they were all thrilled to find romance in their fortunes.

They continued strolling leisurely down the other side of the street where the craft brewery tents were located.

Inga spotted a tent with *Nordic Brewing* as the name. She selected it out of the five tents because of her love for all things Nordic and Viking. In fact, the Viking Ship logo caught her eye first. She walked up to the counter to see the menu more closely.

"What can I get you?"

Inga looked up quickly when she heard the strong Norwegian accented English and to her surprise saw almost a *'Thor'* look alike, only his blonde hair was shorter. He could very well be from Viking blood, she thought. *Tall, muscular, with a chiseled face. Have I just died and gone to Valhalla?*

"What can I get you?" he repeated smiling broadly at her.

"What would you suggest?" she managed to get out. "I've never tried your brand before."

"For you lovely lady, I'd suggest the Viking Blonde Ale."

"Sounds absolutely perfect."

He turned his broad toned back toward her stretching the black T-shirt taut against his muscles and filled a plastic souvenir cup with Valhalla printed on one side and a picture of a Viking on the other side.

Inga pulled a five-dollar bill from her purse and set it on the counter. He handed her the cup instead of setting it down and her fingers lightly brushed his in the process. *There it was again.* A shiver of sorts shimmied its way through her body.

"Thank you, hope you enjoy it," he said as he picked up the money to put in the cash register.

"Thanks, I'm sure I will," Inga said while her eyes lingered on this modern-day Viking man. She felt sad that she would most likely not ever see him again. *Oh well, one can only wish.* She turned and walked away spotting her friends up ahead at a different craft brewery tent.

www.ingramcontent.com/pod-product-compliance
Lightning Source LLC
Chambersburg PA
CBHW022047170626
46808CB00003B/1396